KT-212-607

Map of Friendship Forest

Can you keep a secret? I thought you could!

Then I'll tell you about an enchanted wood.

It lies through the door in the old oak tree,

Let's go there now - just follow me!

We'll find adventure that never ends,

And meet the Magic Animal Friends!

Love

Goldie the Cat

Grace Woollyhop's Musical Mystery

Daisy Meadows

ORCHARD

Honey Tree
Sunshine Meadow
Mr Cleverfeather's Inventing Shed
Goldie's Grotto
Toadstool Cafe
Toadstool Glade
Parasol Tree
Mrs Taptree's Library
Library
Friendship Tree
Grizelda's Workshop
Spark Fall
Rushing Rapids
Entrance to the Caverns
Butterfly Bowery
Nibblesqueak Bakery

Contents

CHAPTER ONE: A Stolen Scarf 9

CHAPTER TWO: The Woollyhop Shop 23

CHAPTER THREE: Hopper's Spell 35

CHAPTER FOUR: The Honey Tree 47

CHAPTER FIVE: Queenie Bumblebuzz 57

CHAPTER SIX: Magic at Harmony Hall 67

CHAPTER SEVEN: A Tower Makeover 79

CHAPTER EIGHT: Secret Singers 93

CHAPTER ONE

A Stolen Scarf

One bright Saturday morning, Jess Forester sat at the kitchen table in the cottage where she lived with her dad. She and her best friend, Lily Hart, were sewing colourful knitted squares together.

"A few more stitches and the blanket will be finished!" said Jess.

Mr Forester came in with a bucket of apples. "How's the knitting going?" he asked as he kicked off his wellies.

Lily and Jess proudly held up their handiwork.

"That's excellent – much better than I could do!" said Mr Forester.

"It's for a foal with a bad cold," said Lily. "He's one of our patients."

Lily lived across the road from

Jess. But her house wasn't just an ordinary home – her parents ran the Helping Paw Wildlife Hospital in a barn in their garden. Both girls adored animals and spent as much time looking after the patients as they could.

"Finished!" said Jess, snipping the last thread. "We'll take it to Helping Paw now. See you later, Dad!"

The girls hurried to the Harts' garden. Although it was sunny, there was a slight chill in the air. Leaves drifted from the trees, and their brilliant autumn colours glowed in the sunlight.

As Jess and Lily hurried past the outside runs, they smiled to see rabbits nibbling crisp lettuce, snoozing squirrels and a cheeky-faced fox cub with a bandaged leg.

"They're warm enough now," said Lily, "but it'll soon get colder. We'd better knit lots more snuggly blankets!"

Before they reached the paddock, they heard a funny sound.

Chooff!

Jess glanced at Lily. "What could that be?" she wondered.

A foal's brown face peered out from a wooden shelter. As he trotted over to the fence, he sneezed. "Chooff!"

"Aww, poor you," said Lily, stroking his soft cheek.

The foal shook his long brown mane. Then he put his nose to the blanket and sniffed.

"He likes it!" said Jess.

They gently laid the blanket over the foal's back, and he whinnied softly.

"He's saying thank you," Lily giggled.

Just then, rustling noises came from a nearby drift of fallen leaves. "Maybe it's a hedgehog," said Jess. "Those leaves are just the sort of place they usually hide in."

But when the leaves shook again, two pointed ears appeared, then out stepped a beautiful golden cat.

"Goldie!" Lily cried.

The cat curled around both their legs, purring happily.

The girls bent to stroke her. Goldie was their magical friend! She'd taken them on lots of adventures in a secret place called Friendship Forest. It was a world where all the woodland animals lived in adorable little cottages and dens. And, best of all, they could talk!

Goldie bounded to the gate.

Jess's eyes sparkled. "She's taking us back to Friendship Forest!"

Goldie led them towards Brightley Stream, at the bottom of the garden. They skipped over the stepping stones that crossed the water, and ran towards a lifeless old tree right in the middle of Brightley Meadow.

The Friendship Tree!

As Goldie reached it, the bare branches burst into life. New leaves sprang from every twig. Two young squirrels raced up and down the tree, gathering their winter hoard of brown acorns, and a trio of trilling bluebirds swooped among the branches, nibbling fat red berries.

Goldie touched a paw to the trunk. Instantly, letters appeared, carved into the bark.

The girls joined hands. Shivering with

excitement, they read the words aloud. "Friendship Forest!"

A small door appeared in the trunk. Jess grasped the leaf-shaped handle and opened it.

Shimmering light shone out as Goldie went inside.

Jess and Lily shared a smile, then followed her into the golden glow. A tingle ran right through

them. They knew that meant they were growing smaller, just a little.

Lily squeezed Jess's hand. "It's so exciting!" she whispered.

The light faded, and the girls found themselves in a beautiful forest clearing. Sunlight shone through the branches and dappled the ground.

It was much warmer than chilly Brightley, and

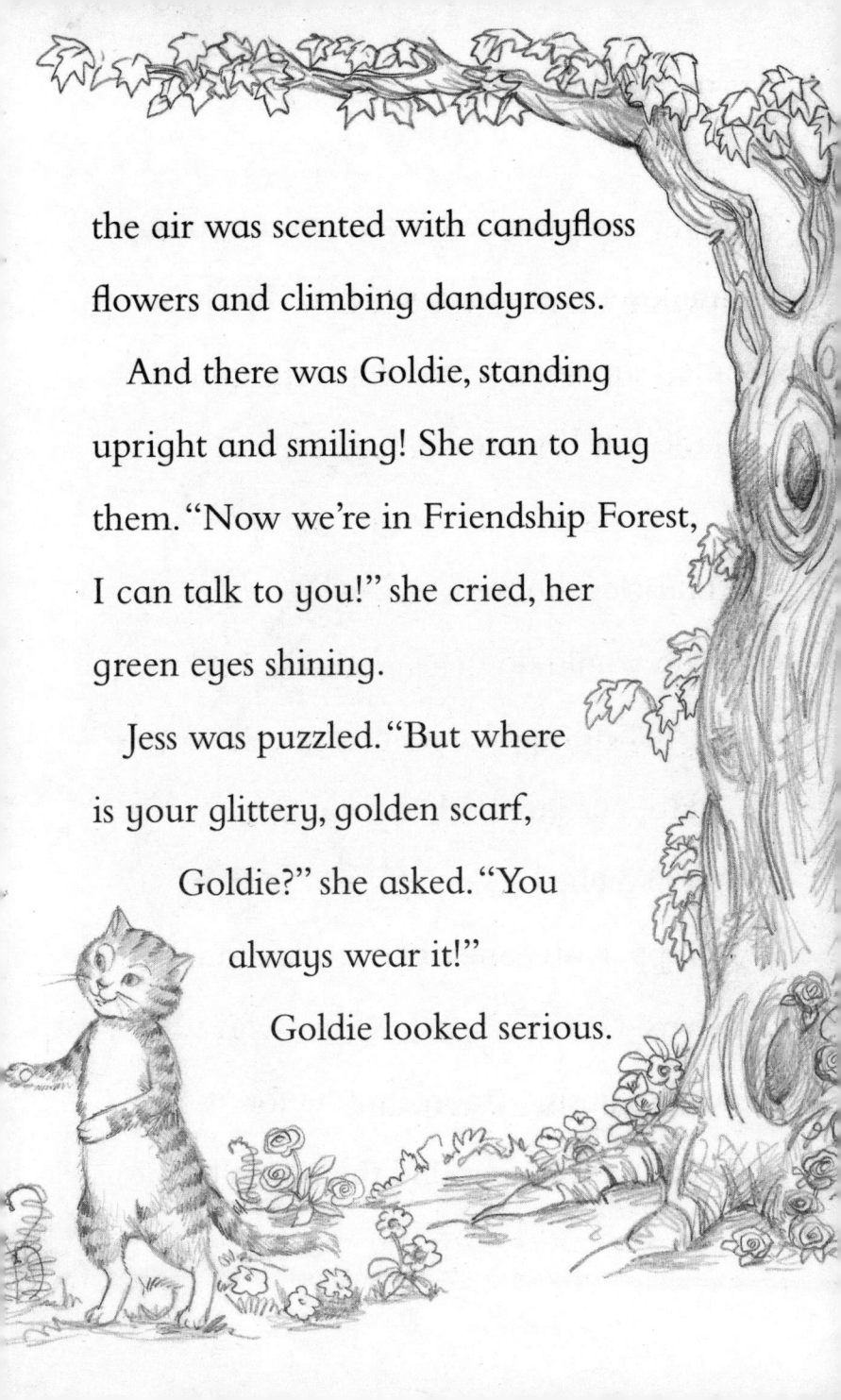

the air was scented with candyfloss flowers and climbing dandyroses.

And there was Goldie, standing upright and smiling! She ran to hug them. "Now we're in Friendship Forest, I can talk to you!" she cried, her green eyes shining.

Jess was puzzled. "But where is your glittery, golden scarf, Goldie?" she asked. "You always wear it!"

Goldie looked serious.

"Someone snatched it and used it to wipe slime over the windows of the Toadstool Café," she said. "I found it in Toadstool Glade, but I'm afraid it's ruined."

Lily was shocked. "Who would do that?" she gasped.

"Hopper the toad," Goldie replied.

Hopper was one of Grizelda's four helpers. Grizelda was a witch who was always causing trouble in the forest. She had found Hopper and the others at the

Witchy Waste, which used to be a lovely water garden, with ponds, streams and flowers, until Hopper and her friends had messed it up. Grizelda had given the four creatures a magic spell which had the power to turn one of the forest animals into a messy creature too. Together they would spoil the forest, just like the water garden. All the good animals would be driven away and Grizelda could have Friendship Forest to herself!

Lily and Jess had already helped stop Peep the bat, Masha the rat and Snippit the crow's spells from working, but

Hopper the toad hadn't cast hers yet.

"The Friendship Forest concert will be at Harmony Hall later today," said Goldie. "I'm worried that Hopper will try to ruin it."

Jess nodded. "I remember Grizelda saying that Hopper is the messiest creature of all."

"You're right," said Lily. "We've got to find Hopper before she casts her spell – or Friendship Forest will be ruined!"

CHAPTER TWO

The Woollyhop Shop

Jess turned to Goldie. "Where did you last see Hopper?" she asked.

"In the place where I got my scarf," said Goldie. "The Woollyhop Shop."

"The Woollyhop Shop?" said Lily, eyes sparkling. "Where's that?"

"I'll show you," said Goldie. "We can

see if that messy toad is still around."

"Maybe we could get you a new scarf while we're there!" said Jess.

The girls hurried after Goldie through the forest to a grassy meadow, dotted with pink daisies and bobbing buttercups. In the centre stood a green-painted barn with a yellow sign over the door.

"The Woollyhop Shop," read Jess. "The

one-stop shop for all your woolly wants!"

They opened the door and peeped inside.

Brightly coloured balls of wool were piled on the shelves. Colourful scarves, hats and jumpers hung on painted hangers. On the counter was a basket labelled, '*Snuggle Socks, for mice, hamsters and newborn kittens!*'

Two sheep stood near a loom with a half-finished pink blanket on it.

A pair of fluffy lambs skipped by, carrying balls of pretty raspberry-pink wool to the loom.

"Hello!" the smaller lamb cried as she

spotted Goldie and the girls.

The other lamb and the two sheep looked up, smiling.

"Welcome to our shop!" the biggest sheep called. "I'm Mr Woollyhop."

The two lambs ran over to Jess and Lily.

"I'm Grace Woollyhop," said the smaller lamb. "That's my big brother Hamish and our Ma and Pa."

Jess grinned. "This is Lily and I'm Jess."

Mrs Woollyhop bustled over. "Can we help you?" she asked.

"We hope so," said Lily. She quickly explained about the creatures from the

Witchy Waste. "Have you seen Hopper the toad nearby? She's been spotted around here."

The Woollyhops shook their heads.

"We haven't seen Hopper, but we'll look out for her," Mrs Woollyhop said.

"Please don't let her in the shop," said Jess. "Hopper's very messy. She might ruin all your lovely wool!"

"She stole Goldie's scarf," added Lily. "May we choose another one for her?"

Grace skipped up and down, her fluffy tail swishing. "We can make a new one on our magical loom!" she cried.

"Magical?" asked Jess.

"Mr Cleverfeather the owl invented it," explained Mr Woollyhop. "It's very fast. We're making fluffy blankets for today's concert, so everyone can be comfy and cosy while they enjoy the show."

Grace showed the girls the loom. It was a wooden frame, with strings stretched across it, like a harp. It had a silver tube and a cone-shaped funnel at the back, and a large tray at the front.

"What colour would you like your scarf to be?" asked Grace.

"Glittering gold, please," said Goldie, "just like my old one."

Hamish tipped balls of sparkling golden wool into the funnel. Then he spoke into the silver tube. "Scarf!"

With a click and a clunk and a *shwoop shwoop shwoop*, the loom began its work. It was so fast that Lily and Jess could hardly see what was happening. Then out of the front appeared a length of golden fabric. It grew and grew until, with a final *shwoop*, the finished scarf dropped into the tray.

"Wow!" Jess gasped.

"That *is* magical!" said Lily.

Grace draped the scarf around Goldie's shoulders.

The girls were just admiring it when Hamish said, "Yuck! What a pong!"

Dirty yellow sparks flew around the loom. Smelly ones!

Jess glanced at Lily and Goldie. They all knew that Grizelda the witch made

smelly sparks!

Click, clunk, shwoop shwoop shwoop went the loom.

"That's funny…" said Hamish. "It's started working without any wool!"

They all watched the magical loom curiously. Soon a woolly purple object dropped into the front tray.

Lily picked it up. "It's a hat!"

"Not just any hat…" added Goldie.

"I think it's a witch's hat!"

"Oh no!" cried Jess. "Grizelda's definitely here somewhere!" As she spoke, something bright caught her eye. "Look!"

An orb of yellow-green light hovered in the doorway, then exploded in a huge shower of stinky sparks.

The sparks cleared to reveal the bony witch, wearing high-heeled, pointy-toed boots, a purple tunic and tight black

trousers. Her green hair swirled around her head like octopus tentacles.

The sheep family huddled behind a rail of woolly jumpers, but Lily, Jess and Goldie bravely faced the wicked witch.

"What do you want, Grizelda?" Jess demanded.

"Ha! The interfering cat and the meddling girls!" the witch snapped. "Well, this time you won't be able to stop my plans! Friendship Forest will be mine!"

CHAPTER THREE

Hopper's Spell

Grizelda snatched the woolly hat and put it on. Her hair dangled limply beneath it like wet seaweed. "Ha haa!" she cackled. "When this shop is mine, I'll make myself new clothes every day!"

Mrs Woollyhop gave a sad bleat from behind the rail of jumpers. "Our shop is for *all* the animals, not just you!" she said.

Grizelda cackled again. "Now the fun starts!" she sneered.

She turned to the girls and clicked her fingers. There was a puff of smoke that smelled like rotting cabbage.

When it cleared, there stood the four creatures from the Witchy Waste – Masha the rat with her tatty straw hat, Snippit the crow in his scruffy waistcoat and Peep the bat with his wonky tie. Hopper the toad, wearing her necklace, waddled towards the girls, leaving a trail of green slime across the floor.

Goldie pulled Jess and Lily away.

Grizelda scowled. "You girls and that cat stopped my other creatures' spells from working, but you won't stop Hopper." She turned to the toad. "Cast your spell!"

Just then a ball of wool rolled out onto the floor in front of the toad. Grace poked her head out from behind the jumpers.

"Oops," she whispered.

"Hide, Grace!" called Goldie.

But it was too late. Hopper had spotted her! The toad sprang towards Grace and she froze, looking terrified.

"Grace, run!" shouted Jess.

But the lamb's legs were shaking too much. "Maa!" she bleated.

Before anyone could move, Hopper's long, flat tongue flicked out. Immediately, purple sparks showered over poor Grace.

"Oh no!" cried Lily. "Hopper's cast her spell. Now Grace will start making messes just like a toad!"

The sparks faded. For a moment, the lamb's sweet woolly face looked surprised. Then she grinned and bounded around the shop, knocking over the rest of the balls of wool that were stacked up in neat piles. They tumbled down and unravelled, making a tangled mess all over the floor.

"Haa!" Grace bleated.

Hopper gave a croaky laugh and Grizelda cackled nastily.

Mr Woollyhop reached out to catch Grace, but she slipped under the loom and out the other side.

"My poor little Grace!" bleated Mrs Woollyhop. "Look what that toad has done to her!"

The Witchy Waste creatures headed for the door, followed by Grace. The girls dived to catch her as she passed, but the little lamb wriggled free, and the five creatures raced outside.

"Go!" Grizelda shrieked. "Make the forest a slimy mess!" She snapped her fingers and disappeared.

Mrs Woollyhop burst into tears.

"Paaaa!" Hamish bleated, "bring Grace back!"

Mr Woollyhop shook his head. "I don't know what to do," he bleated. "She's under a spell."

"Don't worry, we know a spell, too!" said Jess. "It can break Hopper's magic and turn Grace back to her normal self!"

"We used it to help Olivia Nibblesqueak the hamster and Evie Scruffypup," said Lily.

"And Chloe Slipperslide the otter," added Jess. "Let's hope it works for Grace too!" She pulled her little sketchbook from her pocket and read out the spell.

"You want to be yourself again?
Then here's what you must do.
Gather up those favourite things
That mean the most to you.

What do you like to do
the most?
What food do you love
the best?
And what's your
biggest secret?
Now here's a little test.

Put them in your favourite place,
The place you love to be.
If someone names those things aloud,
Yourself once more you'll be."

Hamish put his tiny trembling hoof in Lily's hand. "What does it mean?" he whispered.

"We must find Grace's favourite food," Lily explained, "and something to do with her favourite hobby, and something that shows her biggest secret. We'll gather those in her favourite place and chant the words that will undo Hopper's spell."

Jess tucked her book away. "What's Grace's favourite food?"

The Woollyhops looked at each other – and shook their heads.

"She has a new favourite every week," said Mrs Woollyhop. "Last week it was clover muffins, and the week before that it was buttercup biscuits. So this week it could be anything!"

"I don't know what her secret is either," said Mr Woollyhop sadly.

But Hamish gave a cry. "We do know her favourite hobby, though! It's playing the tambourine. She's really excited about playing in the concert later." His face fell. "At least, she was going to."

Lily hugged him. "We'll make sure she can," she said. "We need Grace's tambourine for the spell!"

"She leaves it at her music teacher's house!" said Hamish. "That's Melody Sweetsong the nightingale," he explained.

Goldie's face lit up. "I know where she lives!" she cried. "Come on!"

"Good luck!" called the Woollyhops as the girls followed Goldie out of the shop.

As they hurried through the trees, they saw a slimy trail where Hopper must have passed. Scraps of raspberry-pink wool were stuck in the green slime.

"What a horrible mess!" said Lily in dismay.

"Hurry!" cried Jess. "We must stop Hopper and Grace, or the forest will be completely covered in slime!"

CHAPTER FOUR

The Honey Tree

The girls followed Goldie through the forest until she stopped, her ears pricked up. "Can you hear that?"

The girls listened.

"That's beautiful," said Jess. "Is it a piano playing?"

Goldie smiled. "No – it's Melody

Sweetsong, she's singing!"

They went on until they reached a silver birch tree, surrounded by flowering bushes that smelled of delicious butterscotch ice cream.

"Here we are," said Goldie, pointing to a little cottage nestling among the lowest branches of the tree. The nightingale's song floated through open windows where feathery curtains fluttered in the soft breeze.

Goldie pulled a rope attached to a bell by the cottage door. When the bell jangled, the singing paused and Melody

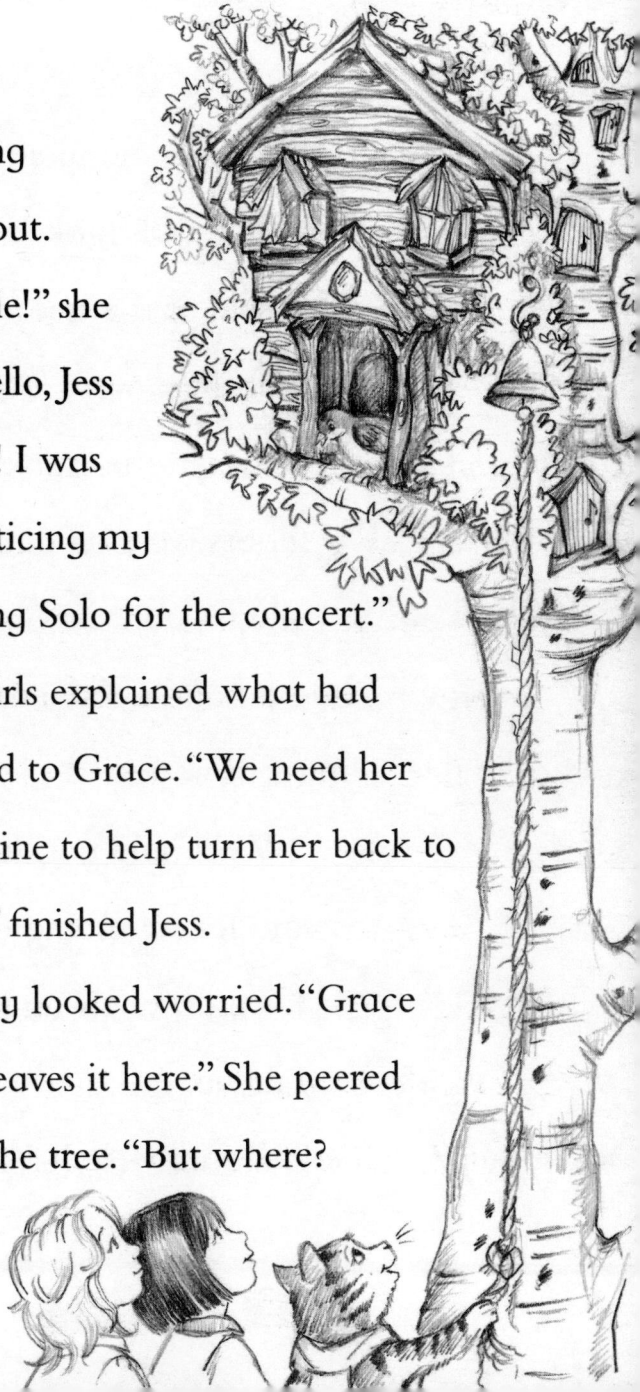

Sweetsong popped out.

"Goldie!" she said. "Hello, Jess and Lily! I was just practicing my Sweetsong Solo for the concert."

The girls explained what had happened to Grace. "We need her tambourine to help turn her back to normal," finished Jess.

Melody looked worried. "Grace always leaves it here." She peered around the tree. "But where?

I have so many cupboards."

The girls looked more closely at the tree, and saw that there were lots of little doors in the trunk. The doors were all different shapes and sizes, and each had a handle shaped like a musical note.

"We'll help you to search," said Jess, climbing on the lowest branch, and helping Lily up.

Goldie and Melody joined

them, opening all the cupboards. Inside each one was a musical instrument. They found little trumpets, banjos, cymbals, and a circle of tiny drums with ten drumsticks.

"That's a bang-a-lot," Melody explained. "The Twinkletail mice love playing it!"

Finally, behind a tall narrow door, Jess spotted a little tambourine. "Look!" she cried out.

"That's Grace's!" said Melody, perching on Lily's shoulder.

"Hooray!" said Jess. She picked it up. "Oh, yuck! More sticky slime!"

Melody laughed. "That's not slime," she said. "It's honey! Grace ate lots of it yesterday before her lesson. Her wool was covered in it when she arrived!"

Lily grinned at Jess. "Honey must be Grace's favourite food right now. Can we get that from the Treasure Tree?"

Melody shook her head, smiling. "No, you need to visit the Honey Tree, near Sunshine Meadow," she said.

The friends climbed down, thanked Melody and set off.

"Good luck!" she trilled after them.

The path was lined with soft grass that tickled their ankles and made them giggle. They reached the red, orange and yellow flowers of Sunshine Meadow, and just beyond that saw the Honey Tree, with a little hive nestling in its lower branches. It had flowery curtains hanging in the windows and a doormat outside.

The air was filled with the buzzing of busy bees, flying in and out of the cottage.

"It's so pretty!" cried Lily. She hurried towards the Honey Tree. But her foot slid on something wet, and she skidded across the ground. Jess reached out to catch her, but she slid, too.

"Eeek!" shrieked Jess, as they both tumbled down.

Lily sat up, examining her hands and knees. "Urgh!" she cried. "Slime!"

Goldie pulled them to their feet, but all three froze when they heard a voice bleating, "Haa haa!"

Hopper and Grace Woollyhop stood beneath a nearby tree, giggling at the girls.

Jess groaned. "Look at Grace's coat! She looks as messy as Hopper already."

The lamb laughed again. "Mess is fun!"

"The best fun!" said Hopper. "We're making the whole forest lovely and slimy!"

She hopped into the trees with Grace bounding after her.

Goldie turned to the girls, looking anxious. "If they carry on," she said, "no one will be able to get around the forest. It'll be too slimy."

Lily nodded. "We must lift that spell!"

"We have to get Grace's favourite food." Jess said. "But how?"

The Honey Tree was completely surrounded by a moat of slippery slime!

CHAPTER FIVE

Queenie Bumblebuzz

The three friends stared in horror at the revolting moat of slime surrounding the Honey Tree.

"How can we get across?" said Goldie. "It's too wide to jump."

Jess looked around desperately for something that might help, and spotted a long fallen branch. "There!" she cried. "Let's use that as a bridge!"

Lily and Goldie took one side of the branch, and Jess the other. Together they lifted it to the edge of the slime and stood it on end.

"Ready?" said Jess. "One…two…three…drop!"

They let the top of the branch fall across the slime.

Gloop!

"I'm good at balancing," said Goldie. "I'll go first to check the branch is strong enough. You don't want to fall into that horrid slime again!"

She ran lightly across, then called back, "It's perfectly steady!"

Lily went first, then Jess, and soon they were safely on a small dry grassy patch close to the tree trunk.

"Hello!" Goldie called up to the cottage.

The fluffiest gold and brown bee they'd ever seen flew down, landing on Goldie's

paw. She wore a tiny golden crown and, when she spoke, her voice was a soft hum.

"I," she said, "am Queenie Bumblebuzz."

Lily explained that they needed honey. "It's to save a little lamb called Grace Woollyhop, Your Majesty—"

"Bzzzzz," Queenie interrupted. "Of course you may have some honey! What sort does Grace like? We have lavender honey, blueberry honey, orange blossom honey and many more. See?" She pointed out lots of little hives dotted around the Honey Tree.

Jess gave a sigh. "They all sound delicious," she said. "But we don't know which one is Grace's favourite."

Goldie's whiskers drooped unhappily. But then Lily gave a cry.

"Yes, we do!" she said, holding out the tambourine. "Grace's favourite honey is all over this!"

Queenie flew over to the tambourine and tasted the sticky honey. "Why it's clover honey," she said. "We've got plenty of that!"

She flew into the hive, and in moments, she came out again with a group of cheerful buzzing bees, who were carrying a little wooden bucket full of golden honey.

"Thanks so much," Jess said, gently taking it from them.

"It's our pleasure to help," said Queenie. "Grace is a dear little lamb. We're looking forward to seeing her at the concert in Harmony Hall."

"Are you going?" asked Lily.

"I am the leader of the royal bee band," said Queenie proudly. "We're called the Honey Buns. We'll be performing the Bumble Boogie!"

"We'll look forward to that!" said Lily. She had a thought. "Queenie, do you know anything about Grace's secret?"

"No," said the bee, "but Buzz Busywing is her friend, and he was behaving very strangely this morning. He left for Harmony Hall, but he wouldn't tell anyone what he was doing. We bees have been buzzing about it all morning - it's a

mystery! Perhaps it could be something to do with Grace's secret?"

"Maybe," Jess said. "We'll go and find him. Thank you, Your Majesty."

The friends made their way back across the branch and through the forest. "Where is Harmony Hall, Goldie?" Lily asked.

"This way!" Goldie led them through the forest, up to a curtain of glossy

green ivy. The sound of sweet voices singing came from behind. "Welcome to Harmony Hall," she said, pulling back the curtain.

"Wow!" said Jess and Lily.

They stepped into a beautiful outdoor theatre. The curved stage was surrounded by stone benches carved from shimmering pink rock that sparkled in the sunlight.

A choir was rehearsing on stage, with wooden stands holding their song sheets.

"Some of our friends are here already!" whispered Jess in delight.

The singers were Lola Velvetnose the mole, Sophie Flufftail the squirrel and Emily Prickleback the hedgehog. Singing along with them was a bee.

"He must be Buzz Busywing," Jess whispered. "That's what the musical mystery was…a choir!"

CHAPTER SIX

Magic at Harmony Hall

"Excuse me, everyone," said Lily, as they looked at the choir of little animals.

Buzz Busywing flew into a spin. "Oh no!" he cried. "Someone's found us! Our surprise will be ruined!"

Lola, Sophie and Emily turned around,

looking wide-eyed, with their paws to their mouths. Then they smiled.

"It's OK, Buzz," called Sophie. "Lily, Jess and Goldie are our friends. They'll keep our secret!"

She bounded over for a hug, with Emily and Lola scurrying after her.

"It's lovely to see you," said Lola, as Lily popped a kiss on her head.

Jess carefully scooped Sophie up.

"That song is a surprise for the concert," the little squirrel explained.

"We're having our last rehearsal before the audience arrives," said Lola.

As the little animals talked excitedly, Lily noticed there were five music stands, but only four singers.

"Who's missing?" she asked.

Lola shuffled her feet and Sophie became very interested in fluffing her tail.

"It's Grace Woollyhop, isn't it?" Jess said. "She's in the choir! That's her secret!"

Sophie, Lola, Buzz and Emily looked at each other anxiously.

"We understand you want to keep Grace's secret," Goldie said gently, "but we really need to know." She explained about Hopper and the spell. "Grace needs our help," she finished.

Sophie and Lola gasped, and Emily's prickles stood up in horror.

"Poor Grace," said Buzz, his wings drooping.

"The only way we can save Grace is by casting a spell," explained Lily. "But first we need to know her biggest secret."

"We'll tell you!" cried Lola. "You're right, singing is Grace's secret. Her family thinks she just plays the tambourine. They don't know that she likes singing too."

"They'll be so surprised," added Lola.

"It's really special for Grace," said Emily, "because she wrote our song, and Harmony Hall is her favourite place."

The girls looked at each other in sheer delight, and Jess planted a kiss on Emily's turned-up nose. "Thanks!" she said. "Now we know Grace's secret is singing, and her favourite place is right here! We've found everything we need to break the spell!"

Just then, Buzz zoomed upwards. "Someone's coming!" he cried.

The ivy curtain swished, and Hopper and Grace appeared. The little lamb was carrying a bucket around her neck, and behind her were all the Witchy Waste creatures.

"Let's slime this place!" said Hopper.

Grace giggled as she sloshed slime from her bucket across the floor.

Masha and Snippit flicked green goo

all over the pink rock seats.

Everyone stared, shocked at the mess.

Buzz fluttered down to rest on Lily's dark hair. "What's happened to Grace?" he buzzed.

"Jess, we have to do the spell now!" said Lily. "We must save Grace and the theatre, or there'll be no concert!"

They darted around horrible puddles of slime as they heaped the tambourine, clover honey and Grace's song sheet on the stage.

"That's everything we need to turn her back into her normal self," said Jess.

The little lamb was helping Hopper spread slime on the stage. Beside them, Peep, Masha and Snippit were giggling with glee.

"Remember the spell," Lily said. "*If someone names those things aloud, yourself once more you'll be.*"

"Grace's favourite hobby," chanted Jess. "Playing her tambourine!"

"Grace's favourite food," Lily added. "Clover honey!"

"Grace's secret!" finished Goldie. "Her surprise song!"

"In Grace's favourite place," they

chanted together. "Harmony Hall!"

Purple sparks flashed all around the little lamb. She suddenly dropped her bucket and looked around. "What's happening?" she asked, and shook herself. Her coat, no longer covered with slime, was as soft and snowy as ever.

"We've done it!" cried Lily.

"Hooray!" cheered the animals.

"I feel so funny," Grace said. "I want my maa!"

The girls rushed to hug her.

"You've been under a spell," said Jess, kissing Grace's sweet little face, "but

you're OK now!"

They heard a miserable croak and turned to see Hopper with her head drooping. Behind her, Peep's wings sagged, Snippit's feathers flopped, and the flower in Masha's hat looked droopier than ever.

"I guess our fun's over," said Peep. "I loved playing with Olivia Nibblesqueak when she was under my spell."

"It was great playing with Chloe

Slipperslide," squawked Snippit.

"And I miss Evie Scruffypup," squeaked Masha.

Hopper looked sadly at Grace. "I'm going to miss playing with Grace too," she said. "I know what will cheer us up. Let's go home to the Witchy Waste, where it's lovely and messy!"

Snippit gave a happy squawk, and jumped in one of the slime puddles. It splashed over Masha and Peep, who squeaked with delight.

Lily couldn't help smiling as she, Jess and Goldie watched the Witchy Waste creatures play. "They're not bad, are they?" she said. "They just really love being messy. No wonder Grizelda thought they would spoil the forest."

Jess nodded. "We ought to teach that horrible witch a lesson," she said. "And I've got an idea how!"

CHAPTER SEVEN

A Tower Makeover

The girls, Goldie and the Witchy Waste creatures watched from a clump of bushes as Grizelda's yellow-green orb floated away from her tower.

"Phew, she's gone!" said Goldie, and they all crawled out of their hiding place.

Jess gazed up at the gloomy tower.

"We'll need a lot of help to make an enormous MESS," she said.

"We'll help!" said Masha.

"And I'll go and fetch some more helpers!" said Goldie, darting away into the trees.

Jess explained the plan to the Witchy Waste creatures. "We're going to make Grizelda's dreary, grey tower a lovely, bright, colourful mess!"

The Witchy Waste creatures squeaked, squawked and croaked with excitement.

Lily laughed. "Everyone start gathering flowers! We want to cover the whole tower in pretty petals!"

"Pretty?" Hopper made a face.

"I mean messy!" Lily said with a grin. The witchy waste creatures nodded.

They'd made a huge heap of flowers around the bottom of the tower when Goldie returned with Olivia Nibblesqueak the hamster, Chloe Slipperslide the otter and Evie Scruffypup. "The butterflies are coming, too," she said.

Peep hugged Olivia with his wings, while Masha squeaked delightedly when she saw Evie. "Hi, Chloe," squawked Snippit, and the otter threw her paws around his feathery neck. Grace, Olivia and Evie wove flower garlands. As each one was finished, Peep and Snippit flew up to drape it between the tower windows.

Masha and Chloe swept petals over the path with their long tails, while Hopper used her slime to stick colourful flowers to the tower's grimy windows.

Goldie dragged out a couple of old cauldrons, and Jess and Lily filled them with flowers, right to the top.

Snippit pecked the words '*Home Sweet Home*' into a piece of bark, and hung it up over Grizelda's creepy-looking door.

Just then, a colourful cloud of butterflies fluttered high up above the roof,

arranging themselves into a beautiful shimmering rainbow.

Everyone stood back to admire the colourful tower. "It looks fantastic!" said Jess. "What a *pretty* mess!"

Goldie nudged her nervously. "Look!"

The familiar yellow-green orb was floating towards them.

"Grizelda!" cried Grace. She ran to hide behind the girls.

The orb exploded into spitting, yellow sparks, and Grizelda appeared. She stared in horror at the beautiful heaps of flowers that lay all around her tower. Her face turned purple with anger.

"My tower!" she shrieked. "It's ruined!"

"See, it's not nice when people change your home," Jess told her.

"It's your doing!" she screamed at them. "You meddlesome, interfering humans!" She turned to glare at the Witchy Waste creatures. "And why haven't you ruined the forest like I told you? You're as much use as cracked cauldrons!"

She stamped in rage and stretched her bony hands towards them.

"Oh no!" Lily gasped. "Quick, we have to distract her!"

"How?" said Jess.

"Grace!" Lily whispered. "Sing!"

The little lamb's voice wobbled at first

but, as she sang, it grew stronger. The sweet sound rang out:

"Always together
Friends are forever
Helping and sharing
Kindness and caring…"

"Everyone sing!" cried Grace, and they all – except Grizelda – joined in the chorus.

"Together forever
Forever together…"

Grizelda clapped her hands over her ears. "Stop that dreadful racket!" she

shrieked, glaring at the Witchy Waste creatures. "You'll never get another magic spell from me. Ever!"

The witch stormed into her tower. As the door slammed behind her, the *'Home Sweet Home'* sign fell down with a *crash*.

"Hooray!" Everyone cheered.

"That was fun!" squawked Snippit.

"I don't think Grizelda will ask you

to do her horrible spells again now," said Goldie, smiling happily.

When Grace and the other the forest animals had hurried away to prepare for the concert, Goldie turned to the girls. "Let's take the Witchy Waste creatures home," she suggested.

Jess held Peep and Snippit's wingtips, and Goldie held Masha's paw. Hopper wiped the slime off her foot on a pile of flowers and took Lily's hand.

They walked along the water's edge to the Witchy Waste. It was in a terrible state, with old boxes, apple cores, rags and all kinds of rubbish everywhere.

The girls stared.

"That's the biggest mess I've ever seen," gasped Lily.

"Isn't it brilliant?" said Snippit proudly.

"We're sorry for causing trouble," said Masha the rat.

"When we said we'd help Grizelda, we didn't realise how mean she was," added Peep the bat.

"That's right," croaked Hopper. "We felt sorry for the forest animals living somewhere so tidy. We thought they'd love some mess."

Lily smiled. "Everything's fine now," she said, "but we must go. We'll come and visit you though!"

The creatures hugged Goldie and the girls, then clambered over the rubbish, into the Witchy Waste.

"We'd better go too," Lily said hurriedly as they all waved goodbye.

"Oh yes," said Jess with a grin.

"We've got somewhere excting to be..."

"Let's hurry to Harmony Hall," Goldie agreed. "It's almost concert time!"

CHAPTER EIGHT

Secret Singers

"Wow!" said Lily. "Harmony Hall is packed!"

Queenie Bumblebuzz flew over to them. "I've saved you some seats," she said, and led Goldie, the girls and the Woollyhop family to the front row. Jess and Lily slid down onto the grass so the Twinkletail mouse family behind them would be able to see.

Mr and Mrs Longwhiskers the rabbits were handing out blackberry and honey ice creams, and Hamish was giving cosy blankets to the animals sitting on the grass. He gave an extra fluffy blue one to the girls.

"They're so soft," said Jess. "Thanks!"

"It's you we must thank," Mrs Woollyhop said to Goldie and the girls, "for saving our little lamb."

"We're so looking forward to seeing

Grace play her tambourine," Mr Woollyhop added.

"Shh!" said Mrs Woollyhop. "The concert's starting."

"They're going to have such a surprise!" Lily whispered to Jess.

Jess nodded, then giggled as Molly and Dolly Twinkletail jumped on to their shoulders for a better view!

The concert began with the Greenhop frogs doing musical acrobatics. There were cheers when Mr Greenhop stood on his head and banged the drum with his feet!

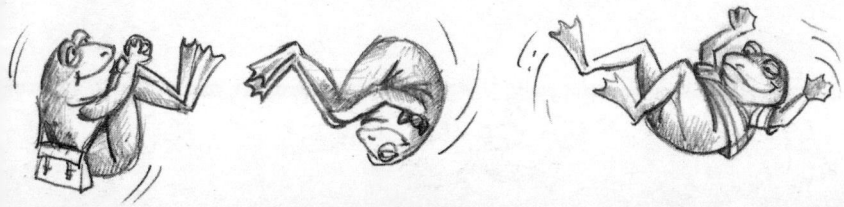

Next, Melody sang her Sweetsong Solo. Just as she finished, there was a great snore from Patch Muddlepup. Melody had sung him to sleep!

The Taptree woodpeckers did an amazing tap dance, wearing little wooden shoes, and then it was time for the Honey Buns.

Queenie Bumblebuzz zoomed onto the stage, followed by the rest of the band. The Bumble Boogie began with a clash of cymbals. In moments, the whole audience was on their feet, clapping along to the lively buzzy beat. The bees flew high in the air to take their bows.

"Where's Grace?" whispered Lily, as Mr Silverback the badger strode on stage.

"A warm welcome, please," he said, "for the Secret Singers, with a song written specially for our concert, called *'Friends Forever'*!"

Grace, Sophie, Emily, Lola and Buzz came on stage to loud cheers.

Jess glanced at the Woollyhops, who were wide-eyed with surprise.

As the group began to sing, Grace's sweet voice filled the theatre.

"Always together,

Friends are forever…"

Mrs Woollyhop's eyes filled with tears. "I never knew she could sing so beautifully," she whispered, as Grace picked up her tambourine and jangled a pretty tune. Buzz hummed alongside her, while Sophie, Emily and Lola danced happily.

When they finished, everyone in the audience clapped.

"What a wonderful surprise!" Mr Woollyhop said.

The concert ended with all the performers singing Grace's song.

"Together forever

Forever together…"

At the end of the song, Grace bounded off the stage, into her parents' arms. They hugged, then Mrs Woollyhop handed Grace a parcel and whispered in her ear.

The little lamb opened the parcel and took out two sparkling pink scarves. She gave one each to Jess and Lily.

"They're a thank you present for helping me and everyone in Friendship Forest," Grace explained. "We made them on our magical loom, so they will never be too hot or too cold. Woollyhop Shop scarves are always just right!"

"Thanks!" said Lily.

"It's so soft!" said Jess.

Goldie admired the scarves. "They're just perfect!"

"Thank you, everyone," said Jess. "The concert was lovely, but it's time for us to go home."

They kissed Grace, and walked with Goldie back to the Friendship Tree.

"Thank you for saving Friendship Forest yet again," said Goldie. "What would we do without you!"

"Let's hope Grizelda's learned her lesson," said Lily.

"Hmm," said Goldie. "Knowing her,

she'll soon come up with a new plan to take over the forest."

"We'll be ready if she does," said Jess, as they reached the Friendship Tree.

"I know you will," said Goldie. She touched a paw to the trunk and the door appeared.

She hugged both girls. "Goodbye!"

"I hope we'll see you soon," Lily said, stepping inside.

"You will, I promise," Goldie called, as they entered the shimmering golden light. "Friendship Forest needs you!"

The glow faded, and the girls found

themselves back in Brightley Meadow. Their cosy new scarves kept them warm in the crisp autumn air.

"What a wonderful adventure," said Jess, as they ran back to the wildlife hospital.

"Look, there's the foal, wearing his blanket," said Lily. "It seems like ages since we saw him!"

They laughed. No time ever passed while they were in Friendship Forest!

The foal trotted to the fence. Lily stroked his nose, and he nibbled at her gorgeous new scarf.

"Hey!" laughed Jess. "You don't need that. You've got your own blanket, silly!"

Lily giggled. "I'm glad our parents know we can knit. We won't have to explain where our scarves came from. They'll think we made them!"

Jess stroked her scarf. "They're a lovely reminder of our animal friends."

The girls shared a smile. They couldn't wait to go back to Friendship Forest!

The End

It's time for the Frost Festival in Friendship Forest, but wicked witch Grizelda wants to spoil the celebrations! Can Jess, Lily and baby bunny Mia stop her?

Find out in the next adventure,

Mia Floppyear's Snowy Adventure

Turn over for a sneak peek . . .

Just then, a tiny figure danced into the clearing, spinning in the air and landing gracefully in front of the girls. It was a little honey-coloured rabbit, wearing a rose-pink tutu. "Ta da!" she said.

"Wow!" Lily said with a smile. "What lovely dancing!"

"I'm Mia Floppyear," said the little bunny. "Hi, Goldie!"

"Hello, Mia," replied Goldie. "This is Lily and Jess."

"I like your tutu," said Jess.

"Thank you," Mia said. Her soft ears flopped over as she curtsied. "It's for my ballet solo at the Winter Show. I'm so excited, I can hardly stand still!" Mia's paws didn't seem to stop moving. She spun on one leg, with the other held out behind her. "Are you going?" she asked.

Before the girls could reply, a familiar yellow-green orb of light floated into the clearing.

"Oh no!" said Goldie. "Grizelda!"

Read

Mia Floppyear's Snowy Adventure

to find out what happens next!

Magic Animal Friends

Read all the Magic Animal Friends adventures and be part of the secret!

Series Three

COMING SOON!

Look out for
Jess and Lily's
next adventure:
Mia Floppyear's
Snowy Adventure

3 stories in 1!

www.magicanimalfriends.com

Puzzle Fun!

Can you help Grace to find the following words in this magical wordsearch?

U	B	Y	X	Z	A	M	S	A	R
E	I	D	L	O	G	S	T	G	A
E	O	F	C	V	N	C	Y	R	H
F	J	Z	V	M	W	A	R	I	G
L	E	Q	W	A	W	R	E	Z	W
W	S	S	Y	G	I	F	M	E	I
S	S	E	W	O	Y	L	I	L	Y
X	H	C	E	P	L	P	Q	D	P
E	J	E	B	T	I	A	R	A	T
J	P	O	H	Y	L	L	O	O	W

WORDS TO FIND:

Scarf
Goldie
Woollyhop
Lily
Jess

U	B	Y	X	Z	A	M	S	A	R
E	I	D	L	O	G	S	T	G	A
E	O	F	C	V	N	C	Y	R	H
F	J	Z	V	M	W	A	R	I	G
L	E	Q	W	A	W	R	E	Z	W
W	S	S	Y	G	I	F	M	E	I
S	S	E	W	O	Y	L	I	L	Y
X	H	C	E	P	L	P	Q	D	P
E	J	E	B	T	I	A	R	A	T
J	P	O	H	Y	L	L	O	O	W

Lily and Jess's Animal Facts

Lily and Jess love lots of different animals – both in Friendship Forest and in the real world.

Here are their top facts about

SHEEP

like Grace Woollyhop

- Sheep have very good memories and can remember at least 50 individual sheep and humans for years.
- Female sheep are called ewes. Baby sheep are called lambs and the noise they make is called bleating.
- There are approximately 900 different breeds of sheep.
- In New Zealand, there are twelve sheep for every one person who lives there.
- A sheep's fur is called wool and has been spun into yarn for over 3,500 years.

Lily's parents aren't the only ones who run a wildlife hospital.

Have you heard of Tiggywinkles – the world's busiest wildlife hospital? They take care of over 10,000 poorly animals every year and treat all kinds of wildlife, including hedgehogs, badgers, birds, foxes and deer.

If you are worried about a wild animal, you can have a look at their website for hints and tips about what to do.

www.tiggywinkles.com

Orchard Books supports Tiggywinkles.

Registered Charity No. 286447 Tiggywinkles,
Aston Road, Haddenham, Aylesbury,
Buckinghamshire HP17 8AF UK
Tel: 01844 292292
Email: mail@sttiggywinkles.org.uk

Magic Animal Friends

Can you keep the secret?

There's lots of fun for everyone at
www.magicanimalfriends.com

Play games and explore the secret world of
Friendship Forest, where animals can talk!

Join the Magic Animal Friends Club!

Special competitions

Exclusive content

All the latest Magic Animal Friends news!

To join the Club, simply go to

www.magicanimalfriends.com/join-our-club/

Terms and Conditions
(1) Open to UK and Republic of Ireland residents only (2) Please get the email of your parent/guardian to enter
(3) We may use your data to contact you with further offers

Full terms and conditions at www.hachettechildrensdigital.co.uk/terms/